Words Along Wires

The story of Alexander Graham Bell

Peter Hepplewhite

*Illustrated by
Alison Astill*

an imprint of Hodder Children's Books

Alexander Graham Bell

3 March 1847 Alexander Graham Bell was born in Edinburgh, Scotland.

1863 Started teaching at Weston House Academy, Elgin, at the age of sixteen.

1866 Studied the works of German scientist Herman von Helmholtz on electricity and acoustics.

1867 *Visible Speech*, a book by Alexander's father Melville, was published.

1870 The Bell family moved to Canada.

1873 Became Professor of Vocal Physiology at Boston University.

1872-4 Worked on ideas for a harmonic telegraph.

1875-6 Invented and tested the telephone.

1876 Showed the telephone at the Centenary Exhibition in Philadelphia.

1878 Married Mabel Hubbard.

1880 Awarded the Volta prize by France (50,000 francs).

1882 Became an American citizen.

1890 Founded the American Association for the Promotion of the Teaching of Speech to the Deaf.

2 August 1922 Died in Nova Scotia at the age of seventy-four.

Chapter 1
Professor Bell's Pupil

I'm an old lady now and I lead a very quiet life. But when I was a girl my teacher was Alexander Graham Bell, a struggling inventor. I had just turned fourteen. The year was 1874 and I was living in Boston.

The first time I saw Professor Bell I did not like him – at all! He was tall, with jet black hair and eyes. He had a big nose and a high sloping forehead. His suit was old-fashioned and he dressed badly. He hardly seemed a gentleman.

Now I think he was really rather handsome, but then I was in no mood to be fair. Papa had sent me to him against my will. Professor Bell was a teacher of 'Vocal Physiology' at Boston University – an expert in speech problems. I was to see him once a week as a private pupil. Papa wanted him to help me speak again.

I could hear perfectly until I was five, then I caught scarlet fever. When the sickness passed my skin was left raw and peeling – and I was completely deaf. My skin healed but my hearing never returned.

Papa took me to the best teachers of the deaf but the news wasn't good.

'Your daughter will soon forget how to make intelligent sounds.'

'Training such a young child to speak would be a waste of time.'

'Far better for her to learn sign language and lip reading.'

So I was given the same education as most 'deaf-mutes' in those days. (Isn't that a horrible term, so blunt and rude? But that's what they called us.) Soon I could sign well and follow a conversation, if people faced me. But sadly, as the years went by, my voice became slurred – until even my own family could only understand a few words.

I thought my parents were happy with
me until the day I caught them talking. As
Papa spoke, I read his lips. 'She is a young
lady, not a child any more. If we can't do
something about Harriet's speech, she'll
never find a husband – or a job.'

When he saw me standing in the doorway he turned his head. But it was too late, I'd understood every word. I ran upstairs and cried for hours.

Chapter 2
Helping Hands

Papa was upset that he'd hurt me. He
tried to explain that all he wanted was for
me to find a kind and rich husband. But I
couldn't forget what he had said. Was my
voice so bad? Was it true that no one
would ever wish to marry me?

Shortly after this Papa saw an advert placed by Professor Bell, seeking new pupils. He began to teach me in the fall and, much to my surprise, I enjoyed it. The professor was a kind and jolly teacher and I remember my first lesson well. He told me that my voice was naturally sweet and that I would soon be proud of it. But first I had to understand how it worked.

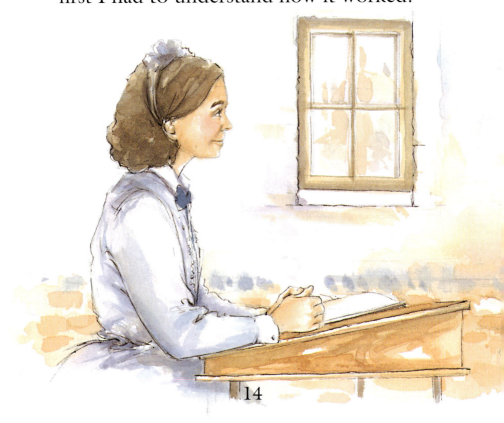

He drew a cut-away view of a face on the blackboard, showing the tongue and the glottis. From this he explained how sounds were made, by the fast vibrations of the vocal cords in the larynx.

Better still, he showed me: placing my
fingertips on his neck, jaw, cheek and lips
to feel the vibrations when he talked.
Then I had to try and make the same
sounds as the professor and feel the
vibrations in my own neck and throat. I
couldn't hear my voice, but I could sense
the noise I was making.

After this I began to learn Visible Speech, a remarkable alphabet devised by his father, Melville Bell. Instead of letters it was a method of writing sounds. This could be any word, in any language, from Japanese to Zulu, and any noise from a sneeze to a roar. Each symbol showed the position of the mouth, tongue, lips and throat to make a distinct sound.

By the fifth lesson Professor Bell had coached me to give my mother a special treat. I rushed home and said clearly: 'I love you, Mama'.

Chapter 3
Professionally Speaking

As the months went by, the professor and
I became friends. He allowed me to call
him by his first name, Alec (short for
Alexander). I told him about Papa's
worries and guess what? He smiled. I was
offended, until he told me his family story.
The smile was one of understanding.

His mother, Eliza, was deaf too, but
this hadn't stopped Melville Bell falling in
love with her. This was back in Edinburgh,
Scotland. (Papa told me that Professor Bell
had a fine Scottish accent.) Alec was born
in 1847, the second of three boys. In spite
of her deafness Eliza taught her sons all
their lessons until they were ten – every-
thing from Latin to music.

Alec learned how the voice works from his father and grandfather. For two generations the Bells had earned their living by helping people with speech problems. By the time he was sixteen Alec was a student teacher of elocution – and younger than some of his pupils!

In 1866 the family moved to London and Alec worked with his father using Visible Speech to teach the deaf. He even trained his dog, Trouve, to speak. By holding the dog's mouth and throat Alec got him to growl – 'ow, ah, ooh, ga, ma, ma'. Put the growls together and what is Trouve saying? 'How are you grandmama?'

In 1870 the Bells decided to start a new
life in Canada. Alec's brothers had both
died of tuberculosis and Alec himself was
often ill. As Melville hoped, the outdoor
life of Ontario was good for his son. A year
later Alec was offered a job in America at
the Boston School for Deaf-Mutes and
began work at Boston University in 1873.

Chapter 4
Harmonics and Love

I soon realized that the professor was under great stress. Often he came to lessons looking worn-out and untidy, as if he had hardly slept. And what a story he told me each time we met! Alec may have been a teacher by day, but at night he was an inventor.

In those days the electric telegraph was the wonder of the age. Messages could be sent almost instantly, as electrical signals along thousands of miles of wires. In 1866 a cable had even been laid on the seabed of the Atlantic, linking Britain and the USA. Alec's idea was stunning – a system to send several messages over the same wire at the same time. It could make the cable companies – and the inventor – a fortune.

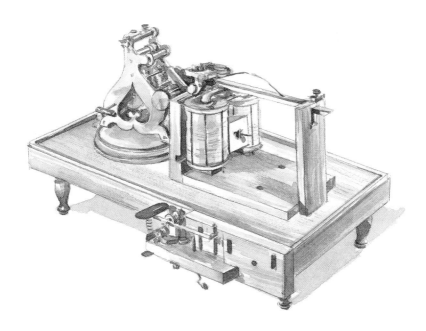

The professor had always been interested in the science of sound. In 1872 he had made a device to help his pupils say two of the hardest letters, 'P' and 'B'.

'If I could trace the patterns of my voice on a piece of smoked glass,' he explained, 'I could show them what the sound looked like. They could then practise with their own voices to make the same pattern.'

This idea depended on 'sympathetic vibration'. Alec demonstrated this principle to me using a piano. When he sang into the instrument, the one string that had the same pitch as his voice vibrated, while all the others kept still.

Likewise, on his 'speech writer' he found that the metal strips (or reeds), needed to trace the pattern, only 'picked up' one tone of his voice. Reeds of different lengths were needed for different tones.

This was Alec's inspiration, a 'harmonic telegraph!' Tuned reeds at both ends of the wire could transmit and receive six or more messages at the same time – if they were sent in different tones. It was ingenious, but he had little money to buy the equipment and pay for the experiments. Then romance came to the rescue!

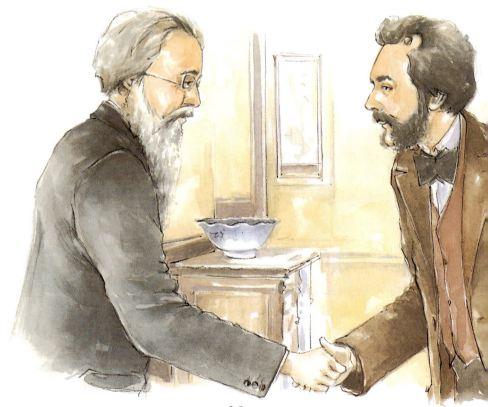

Alec had fallen in love with another of his pupils, Mabel Hubbard. I knew her and was more than a little jealous. She was two years older than me and very beautiful. He confided in her father, a rich businessman, and Mr Hubbard agreed to back him. He would pay for the workshop and equipment, in return for a share of the patent rights.

Chapter 5
The Telephone

1875 was a hard year for poor Professor Bell. With the help of a young assistant, Thomas Watson, he carried out test after test. But his inquiring mind was whirling again. If they could send tones along a wire, then why not words? After all, speech was just a mixture of tones.

Alec explained to Thomas: 'If I could make an electric current vary in intensity, precisely as the air varies in density when a sound passes through it, I should be able to transmit any sound telegraphically, even the sound of speech.'

The first breakthrough came on 2 June –
because of a mistake. The inventors set up
a telegraph circuit between two rooms.
Alec was in the transmitter room with three
sending reeds, while Thomas sat with the
receiver. When one of the steel reeds at
Thomas's end got stuck, he pinged it free
with his finger.

Suddenly Alec let out a delighted yell. The matching reed at his end had received the signal and twanged faintly. The sound had been turned into electricity, sent along the wire, and turned back into sound. At that moment the telephone was born.

Surprisingly Mr Hubbard was not pleased. He warned his young partner to forget about the telephone – or forget about marrying Mabel! Alec was frantic with worry and stopped work on his new invention for weeks. He was so tired that he gave up most of his pupils and I am sure it was only our friendship that led him to keep me. I think our talks were a comfort to him.

Yet most family rows pass and so did this one. By October Mr Hubbard had been won over, and the young couple became engaged.

Mr Hubbard changed his mind about the 'speaking telephone' too and did Alec a great service. On 14 February 1876 he presented the specifications for the telephone to the Patent Office in Washington.

In an almost unbelievable coincidence, Elisha Gray, Alec's great rival, submitted his schemes only hours later. The court battle to decide who was the real inventor of the telephone lasted years.

I can still recall the hectic pace
in Alec's workshop that spring.
Every lesson he told me how
he had improved this or that
part of his design.

'Harriet, when we speak, the sound makes waves in the air,' he explained. 'The diaphragm, a thin metal plate in the mouthpiece of the telephone, picks these up and vibrates, just like an eardrum. An electro-magnet attached to the diaphragm changes these vibrations into electric signals and sends them along the wires. At the other end the receiver turns the signals back into sound.'

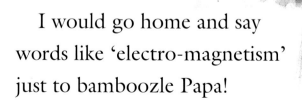

I would go home and say words like 'electro-magnetism' just to bamboozle Papa!

Finally, on Friday 10 March, Alec made the first successful test. Beaming, he told me:

'Harriet, I shouted into the mouthpiece: "Mr Watson – Come here – I want to see you." To my delight he came and declared he had heard and understood what I said.'

Chapter 6
Goodbye to a Friend

That summer my family moved to Chicago.
I missed Alec, but my own quiet life
blossomed. I found a new teacher who
used the 'Bell method' and my speech
continued to improve.

When I was eighteen another modern invention helped me find a job, the type-writer. I worked in an attorney's office, one of the first female clerks the firm employed. And there I met your grandfather. He was not as rich as Papa would have liked, but he was kind! And, just like Eliza Bell, my deafness wasn't important to him.

And Professor Bell? We wrote, and through his letters, and my newspaper scrapbook, I kept up with his whirlwind life. In July 1876 he demonstrated the telephone at the Centenary Exhibition in Philadelphia, in front of Emperor Dom Pedro of Brazil. The emperor was amazed. 'My God,' he said. 'It talks.'

Soon telephone lines were spreading across the country. The Bell Telephone Company was founded in 1877 and the first exchange opened in New Haven, Connecticut, in 1878.

Now, as I sit here in my armchair, remembering all this, I only have one regret. I've never been able to use the telephone myself. Yet this doesn't upset me; I know that it was his work with deaf people that inspired Alexander Graham Bell to send words along wires.

Glossary

diaphragm a thin, flexible skin that vibrates in response to sounds

electro-magnet a piece of soft iron wrapped in a coil of wire; when electricity is passed through the wire the iron becomes a magnet

elocution speaking well

fall American word for autumn

glottis the opening at the upper end of the windpipe

larynx voice box

patent a description of an invention registered with the authorities to show who thought of it first

physiology the science of living things; vocal physiology is about how the voice works

reed vibrating metal plate, in Bell's harmonic telegraph

telegraph electric signalling system invented by William Cooke and Charles Wheatstone in 1837